# Franklin Says Sorry

From an episode of the animated TV series *Franklin*
produced by Nelvana Limited, Neurones France s.a.r.l.
and Neurones Luxembourg S.A.

Based on the *Franklin* books by
Paulette Bourgeois and Brenda Clark.

TV tie-in adaptation written by Sharon Jennings
and illustrated by Nelvana.
TV script written by Nicola Barton.

Kids Can Press Ltd.
29 Birch Avenue
Toronto, Ontario, Canada
M4V 1E2

Printed in Hong Kong by Wing King Tong Company Limited

CDN PA 99 0 9 8 7 6 5 4 3 2 1

**Canadian Cataloguing in Publication Data**

Franklin says sorry
Based on characters created by Paulette Bourgeois and Brenda Clark.

ISBN 1-55074-712-6 (bound)    ISBN 1-55074-714-2 (pbk.)

I. Bourgeois, Paulette.    II. Clark, Brenda.

PS8550.F727 1999    jC813'.54    C99-931360-6
PZ7.Fr 1999

Kids Can Press is a Nelvana company

# Franklin Says Sorry

*Based on characters created by*
*Paulette Bourgeois and Brenda Clark*

Kids Can Press

FRANKLIN had lots of friends and knew how to be a good friend himself. He knew it was important to share his toys and keep his promises. He had learned how to be a good loser and a gracious winner. And one day, Franklin learned how important it is to say sorry.

Franklin and his friends had spent the morning searching through attics and basements, toyboxes and recycling bins. They had been collecting things to turn their tree fort into a ship.

Franklin held up an old cap. "Here's our captain's hat."

"And this can be our telescope," said Bear, holding a bottle to his eye. "Shiver me timbers!" he cried. "A sea monster!"

"I'm not a sea monster," sniffed Beaver. "I'm the mermaid who guards the sunken treasure."

"Okay, maties," said Franklin. "Let's make this fort shipshape!"

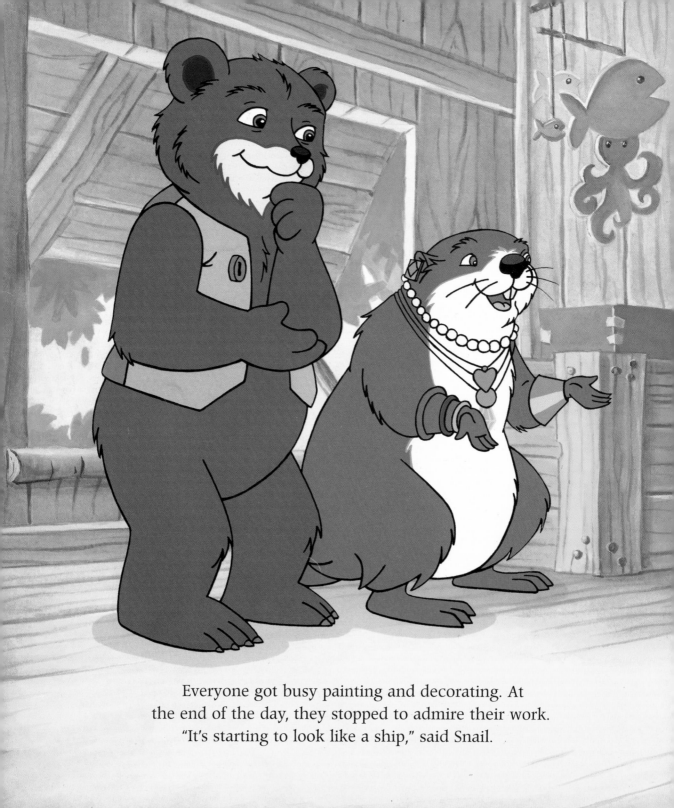

Everyone got busy painting and decorating. At
the end of the day, they stopped to admire their work.
"It's starting to look like a ship," said Snail.

"But it still needs something," sighed Beaver.
"Something special," added Bear, thoughtfully.
The friends agreed to work again in the morning.

The next day, Franklin met Bear on his way to the tree fort. Bear was carrying a shoebox.

"What's in the box?" asked Franklin.

Bear hid the box behind his back. "I can't tell you," he said.

Franklin was puzzled. "Why not?" he asked.

"It's a secret," explained Bear. "You'll find out when everyone's at the fort."

"Please, Bear," begged Franklin. "I won't tell."

"Well … all right," Bear finally agreed. "But not here."

Franklin and Bear hurried to the tree fort. Bear checked to make sure no one else was around. Then he opened the shoebox and carefully took out a flag. On it was a ship and a rainbow.

"A flag!" exclaimed Franklin. "It's just what our ship needs."

"I made it all by myself," Bear said proudly. "I want to fly it from a branch and surprise the others. But first I have to find some string."

Bear hid the flag under a bucket and climbed down the ladder.

"Remember, Franklin," he called. "Don't tell anybody."

Franklin was taping up portholes when Fox arrived.

"I found a ship's wheel," announced Fox.

"Great!" said Franklin. "And Bear brought something really special."

"What?" asked Fox.

"I can't tell," answered Franklin. "It's Bear's secret."

"You can tell me," said Fox. "I'm Bear's friend, too."

Franklin thought for a moment.

"Please," begged Fox.

"I guess it'll be okay," Franklin said slowly. "But you can't tell anyone else."

"I can keep a secret," Fox replied.

Franklin took the flag from its hiding place.

"That really *is* special!" exclaimed Fox.

"Bear's going to show everyone later," Franklin explained, "so we have to keep it a secret."

"I will," said Fox. "Don't worry."

Franklin put the flag back.

"I'll see you after lunch, Fox," he said. "Remember, don't tell anybody."

That afternoon, Bear stopped by Franklin's house.
"I found some string," said Bear. "Now I can put
up my flag and show the others."
    But when Bear and Franklin arrived at the tree
fort, they found Fox already showing the flag to
Beaver and Snail.

"Fox!" cried Franklin. "I told you not to tell anyone."

Bear glared at Franklin. "I told *you* not to tell anyone."

"But Fox said he would keep it a secret," Franklin argued.

"*You* were supposed to keep it a secret, Franklin," replied Bear.

"I want my flag back now. I'm leaving!"

"Wait, Bear," begged Franklin. He grabbed the flag.

"Let go!" said Bear as he gave a hard tug.

Everyone heard a horrible ripping sound.

The flag tore in half.

"That's the last time I tell you a secret, Franklin."
Bear threw down the flag and stomped off.

Everyone stared at Franklin.

"I've never heard Bear talk to anyone like that
before," said Snail.

"I'm glad *I* didn't tell anybody," added Beaver.

Franklin looked worried. "I'd better go talk to
Bear," he said.

   But Bear didn't want to talk to Franklin. No matter what Franklin did, Bear ignored him.

   The next morning, Franklin told Snail all about it.

   "Bear doesn't want to be my friend anymore," Franklin said sadly. "I went to his house, but he closed the door on me. I tried to go bike riding with him, but he rode away. And I did a special trick for him at the pond, but he didn't even smile."

"Did you tell him you're sorry, Franklin?" asked Snail.

"I told him I didn't mean to tell his secret. I told him I'd never do it again," said Franklin.

"But did you say sorry?" Snail repeated.

Franklin started to say something, but then stopped. For a minute he said nothing.

"No," Franklin finally answered. "I never said sorry. But I really am. How can I get Bear to listen to me?"

"We'll think of something," said Snail.

By the afternoon, Franklin and his friends had a plan. First, they taped the flag back together and hung it from a branch. Then they waited quietly in the tree fort, hoping that Bear would come to get his flag. Sure enough, it wasn't long before Bear arrived.

"Hello, Bear," said Franklin. "I have something to say to you."

"I just came for my flag," replied Bear.

"Please listen to Franklin," pleaded Fox.

"Why should I?" asked Bear.

"Because we miss you," said Beaver and Snail.

Bear sighed. "All right," he said.

Franklin took a deep breath.
"I'm sorry, Bear. I am very sorry I told your secret," he said. "Please give me another chance."
Bear looked at Franklin for a long time. Then he smiled and held out his hand.
Everyone cheered.

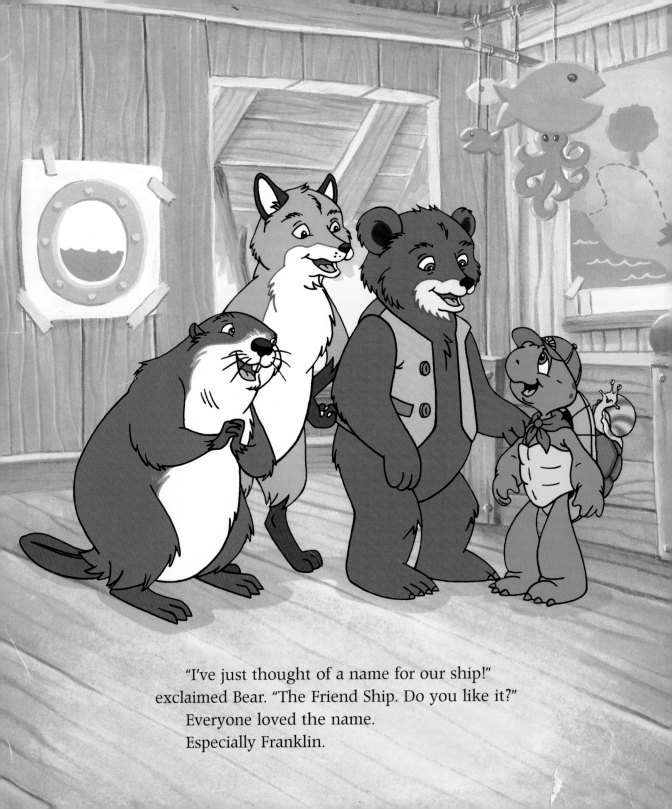

"I've just thought of a name for our ship!"
exclaimed Bear. "The Friend Ship. Do you like it?"
Everyone loved the name.
Especially Franklin.